D0065217

Thanksgiving Day

by Mari C. Schuh

Consulting Editor: Gail Saunders-Smith, Ph.D.

Consultant: Melodie Andrews, Ph.D.
Associate Professor of Early American History
Minnesota State University, Mankato

Pebble Books

an imprint of Capstone Press
Mankato, Minnesota

Pebble Books are published by Capstone Press,
151 Good Counsel Drive, P.O. Box 669, Mankato, Minnesota 56002.
www.capstonepress.com

1 2 3 4 5 6 08 07 06 05 04 03

Library of Congress Cataloging-in-Publication Data
Schuh, Mari C., 1975–
    Thanksgiving Day / by Mari C. Schuh.
    p. cm.—(National holidays)
    Summary: Simple text and photographs describe the history of Thanksgiving
Day and how it is celebrated.
    Includes bibliographical references and index.
    ISBN-13: 978-0-7368-1654-0 (hardcover)
    ISBN-10: 0-7368-1654-2 (hardcover)
    ISBN-13: 978-0-7368-6090-1 (softcover pbk.)
    ISBN-10: 0-7368-6090-8 (softcover pbk.)
    1. Thanksgiving Day—Juvenile literature. 2. Thanksgiving Day—History—
Juvenile literature. [1. Thanksgiving Day.] I. Title. II. Series.
GT4975.S38 2003
394.2649—dc21   2002010636

Note to Parents and Teachers

The National Holidays series supports national social studies standards
related to understanding events that celebrate the values and principles of
American democracy. This book describes and illustrates Thanksgiving
Day. The photographs support early readers in understanding the text. This
book also introduces early readers to subject-specific vocabulary words,
which are defined in the Words to Know section. Early readers may need
assistance to read some words and to use the Table of Contents, Words to
Know, Read More, Internet Sites, and Index/Word List sections of the book.

Table of Contents

Thanksgiving Day 5
History 9
Celebrating 15

Words to Know 22
Read More 23
Internet Sites 23
Index/Word List 24

November

S	M	T	W	T	F	S
						1
2	3	4	5	6	7	8
9	10	11	12	13	14	15
16	17	18	19	20	21	22
23	24	25	26	27	28	29
30						

Thanksgiving Day is the fourth Thursday in November.

Thanksgiving Day is
a day for people to be
thankful for all they have.

Long ago, American Indians had harvest festivals. They were thankful for their crops. They always shared what they had.

The Pilgrims came
to America in 1620.
The American Indians
helped the Pilgrims plant
crops and find new food.

The Pilgrims soon had
a big harvest. The Pilgrims
and the American Indians
celebrated by sharing
a meal.

Today, families and friends celebrate Thanksgiving with a big meal.

Some people eat turkey, cranberries, and pumpkin pie. They tell each other what they are thankful for.

Some people decorate their homes with corn and pumpkins. These decorations remind them of the harvest from long ago.

Thanksgiving Day is
a day to give thanks.

⭐ Words to Know

American Indians—the first people who lived in North America and South America or their descendants

celebrate—to do something fun on a special occasion

cranberry—a small, tart berry that grows on small bushes in wet ground

crop—a plant grown in large amounts; most crops are food.

decorate—to use or add items to make something look nice

festival—a celebration or a holiday

harvest—to gather crops

Pilgrims—a group of settlers who sailed to America from England in 1620

Read More

Ansary, Mir Tamim. *Thanksgiving Day.* Holiday Histories. Chicago: Heinemann Library, 2002.

Marx, David F. *Thanksgiving.* Rookie Read-About Holidays. New York: Children's Press, 2000.

Merrick, Patrick. *Thanksgiving Turkeys.* Holiday Symbols. Chanhassen, Minn.: Child's World, 2000.

Schuh, Mari C. *Thanksgiving.* Holidays and Celebrations. Mankato, Minn.: Pebble Books, 2002.

Internet Sites

Track down many sites about Thanksgiving. Visit the FACT HOUND at *http://www.facthound.com*

IT IS EASY! IT IS FUN!

1) Go to *http://www.facthound.com*

2) Type in: 0736816542

3) Click on "FETCH IT" and FACT HOUND will find several links hand-picked by our editors.

Relax and let our pal FACT HOUND do the research for you!

Index/Word List

America, 11
American
   Indians, 9,
   11, 13
celebrate,
   13, 15
corn, 19
cranberries,
   17
crops, 9, 11
decorate, 19
families, 15
food, 11

friends, 15
harvest
   festivals, 9
harvest, 13,
   19
helped, 11
homes, 19
meal, 13, 15
November, 5
people, 7,
   17, 19
Pilgrims,
   11, 13

plant, 11
pumpkin pie,
   17
pumpkins, 19
share, 9, 13
tell, 17
thankful, 7,
   9, 17
thanks, 21
Thursday, 5
turkey, 17

Word Count: 132
Early-Intervention Level: 14

Credits
Heather Kindseth, series designer; Molly Nei, book designer; Gene Bentdahl,
illustrator; Karrey Tweten, photo researcher

Capstone Press/Gary Sundermeyer, cover, 18; Jim Foell, 1, 4, 14, 20
Corbis/Berstein Collection, 12; Jose Luis Pelaez, Inc., 16
North Wind Picture Archives, 8, 10
Unicorn Stock Photos/Tom McCarthy, 6